I know the sun will shine for me

again another day.

That's what you have taught me,
and I believe in you!

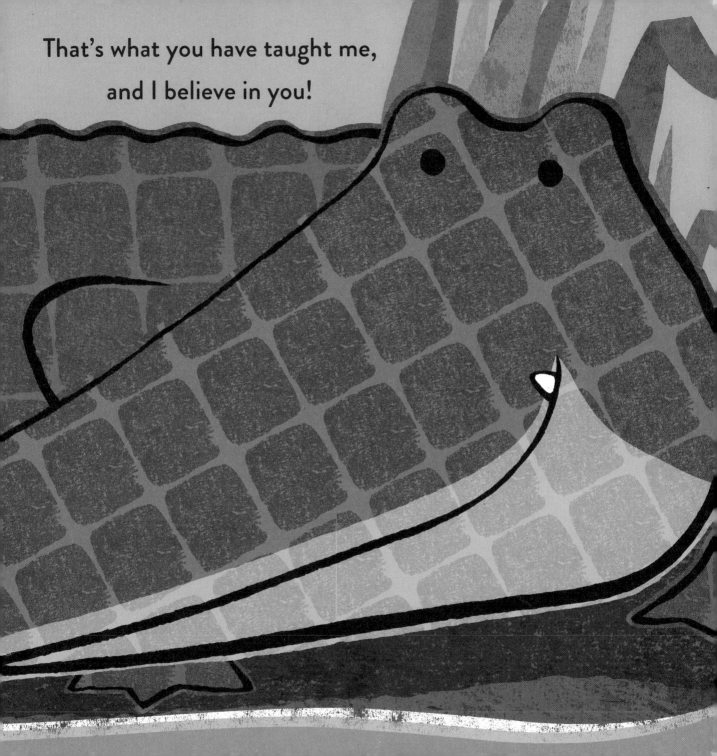

I believe in me,
and though I may be small,

I hold my head up high
as if I'm ten feet tall.

I believe in me.
I'm as good as all the rest.
I know I can do anything
if I just try my best.

I believe in me,
and if anything goes wrong,
I'll never, ever give up;
I'm learning to be strong.

I believe in me,

and if the clouds are grey . . .

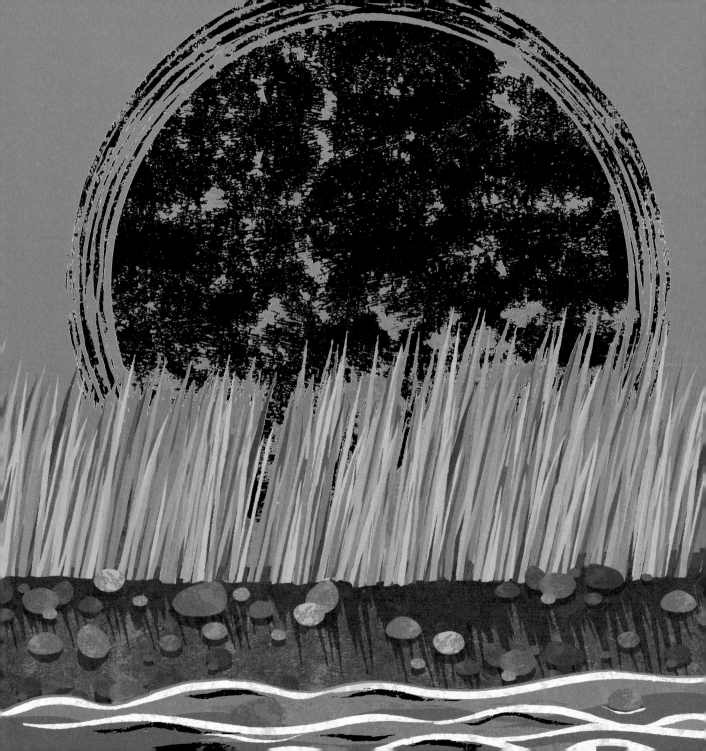

I believe in me,
and when the path gets tough,

I always keep on going
because I am enough.

I believe in me.
I'm reaching for the sky.
Everything is possible
if I'm brave enough to try.

I believe in me,
and you are my biggest fan.
Every time I think I can't,
you tell me that I can!

As I look into your eyes,
that's when I can see . . .